Spooked
PHILIP WOODERSON

Illustrated by
JANE COPE

CHILLERS

The Blob Tessa Potter and Peter Cottrill
Clive and the Missing Finger Sarah Garland
The Day Matt Sold Great-grandma Eleanor Allen and Jane Cope
The Dinner Lady Tessa Potter and Karen Donelly
Ghost from the Sea Eleanor Allen and Leanne Franson
Hide and Shriek! Paul Dowling
Jimmy Woods and the Big Bad Wolf Mick Gowar and Barry Wilkinson
Madam Sizzers Sarah Garland
The Real Porky Philips Mark Haddon
Sarah Scarer Sally Christie and Claudio Muñoz
Spooked Philip Wooderson and Jane Cope
Wilf and the Black Hole Hiawyn Oram and Dee Shulman

PUFFIN BOOKS

Published by the Penguin Group
Penguin Books Ltd, 27 Wrights Lane, London W8 5TZ, England
Penguin Books USA Inc., 375 Hudson Street, New York, New York 10014, USA
Penguin Books Australia Ltd, Ringwood, Victoria, Australia
Penguin Books Canada Ltd, 10 Alcorn Avenue, Toronto, Ontario, Canada M4V 3B2
Penguin Books (NZ) Ltd, 182–190 Wairau Road, Auckland 10, New Zealand

Penguin Books Ltd, Registered Offices: Harmondsworth, Middlesex, England

First published by A&C Black (Publishers) Ltd 1994
Published in Puffin Books 1996
1 3 5 7 9 10 8 6 4 2

Chapter One

Dad called it a secret drawer. It certainly was very odd, slotting into the base of the old chest so you'd never have known it was there. No knob, no handle, no keyhole; no means of pulling it open. I tried to jiggle it loose, but the drawer fitted much too tightly.

I managed to tip the chest forward, hoping the drawer might slide out, and then I noticed a chink – a key-shaped hole in the wood that I hadn't noticed before. A tiny piece of wood had fallen out onto the carpet. The drawer had never been jammed. It had a hidden lock.

Chapter Two

I'd found the chest in Dad's workshop
and wanted it straight away. It was just
the right size for hiding my heaps of old
horror comics, the ones that Mum would
have liked to chuck straight into the bin.
She thought they were gruesome. They
were. But that was the point and I loved
them. They'd feel at home in that chest.

My dad deals in furniture. He buys old broken-down stuff, makes it as good as new and sells it from his "showroom" – what used to be our front lounge.

The chest was still as he'd found it, cob-webbed and riddled with worm-holes.

When I tilted the chest, something kept sliding about. So I went down to Dad's workshop and borrowed his bunch of spare keys.

I tried the keys, one after another. It took about twenty minutes to find an old key that would fit. When I twisted it round, the lock clicked!

I pulled, the drawer slid out and I found myself looking down at a bulky, oblong parcel wrapped in dusty brown paper.

Inside was a musty old copy of *Peter Pan*. Just my luck! I couldn't stand Peter Pan. I thumbed through its yellowy pages and out slipped a bit of brown card.

It was just an old photograph of a girl wearing old-fashioned clothes, but when I turned it over I saw what looked like a message written in wavery letters. I read it. I read it again and a shiver went right down my spine.

Chapter Three

I'm stuck here. I'm lonely and ill. Please come and rescue me. I wait every night and keep hoping. With lots of love
Lisa.

Was Lisa the girl in the photo? I studied her face. She looked solemn and worried and not very well. But what could I do? Not a lot. Her note must have been in the book for goodness knows how long. I would be years too late.

That's what gave me the creeps. Had *anyone* gone to her rescue?

It was Sunday; roast chicken for lunch, yet somehow I didn't feel hungry. I didn't let on to Dad that I'd managed to open the drawer, but I did ask a few careful questions about the chest's previous owner.

Gone into an old people's home. I had to clear out the whole house. She'd lived in the place all her life and never thrown anything out.

"Where is this big house?" I said calmly.

Dad looked a bit disappointed. "Oh . . . off the end of the High Street." He helped himself to more gravy. "Twenty-two Rosewood Gardens. It needs a lot of work done, but it could make four nice flats."

"I'm not going to buy it," I said.

"So what are your plans?" said Mum.

"Ah well. . . ."

I'm sure you've guessed.

As soon as I'd helped to clear the dishes, I slipped out of the kitchen door. In the street it was drizzly and grey, and I started sneezing.

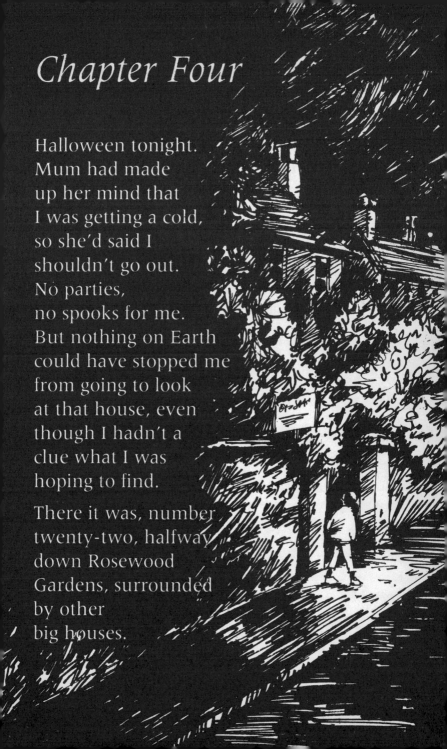

Chapter Four

Halloween tonight.
Mum had made
up her mind that
I was getting a cold,
so she'd said I
shouldn't go out.
No parties,
no spooks for me.
But nothing on Earth
could have stopped me
from going to look
at that house, even
though I hadn't a
clue what I was
hoping to find.

There it was, number
twenty-two, halfway
down Rosewood
Gardens, surrounded
by other
big houses.

I ought to have taken one look, turned round and gone back home. Instead I kept on looking. After a while I noticed a light, a very faint, watery light, in a second-floor window.

Something was moving up there. It flitted across the ceiling. A shadow?

I waited and watched.

Chapter Five

I waited a very long time.

The rain came down in sheets. Water got inside my collar and dribbled down my back. I shivered, I sneezed, I felt awful and wished I was home in the warm. But still I stood there, staring, until that gloomy window was printed on my brain.

I blinked. I shook my head. And that's when I actually saw her.

She moved up close to the window. She pressed her nose to the glass. And though she was far away, she looked like the girl in the photo. She wore the same sort of dark dress with a wide, white, floppy collar buttoned up under the chin.

She lifted a hand and beckoned, as if she wanted my help.

I didn't hang on to wave back. I have to admit it, I bolted.

Chapter Six

Safely back home in my bedroom, I looked at the photo again. Had the girl at the window been Lisa?

The photograph was ancient, the girl had been far away and it had been dark and rainy. But someone had been at the window, alone in the empty house. Why?

I read the note again.

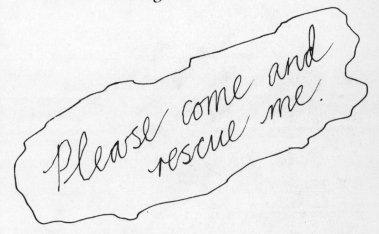

Please come and rescue me.

What if the girl at the window had found the old photo, written the note on the back and hidden it inside the chest? So when the house was cleared, her note would be smuggled out and someone like me would read it?

But why on Earth would she try that, unless she was stuck there – a prisoner!

What I needed were facts, and only Dad could supply them.

Chapter Seven

I knew where to find Dad. He was down in his workshop as usual, mending an old rocking chair. I asked him about the old lady who'd lived at Rosewood Gardens.

"Ah, Mrs Tatley," Dad nodded. "Yes, she'd have liked this chair . . . though come to think of it, Pete, she sold it to me in the first place."

"Yes Dad, but what was she like?"

Bright as a button. In fact she was saner than I am.

Not so impressive, I thought. If she had been Dracula's sister, Dad would still have been fooled. She must have acted the harmless old dear and chuckled at all his bad jokes.

I tried another line. "She can't have been all alone, Dad, not in that great big house?"

"Course she was," Dad said gruffly. "That's why she had to move out." But then, in a gentler tone, he said,

She'll be all right, Pete. She's got some family. Her children are old themselves now, but they've got grown-up kids with nice little kids of their own, and they live on the far side of town, see? Quite close to the old people's home.

"Oh . . . good," I said. "So you're sure then, that nobody's left in the house. You looked all round when you cleared it, right up in those top floor bedrooms?"

Dad gave me a curious glance. "That's where I found your chest, Pete."

"Front bedroom, on the left? The one with the small narrow window?"

"That's it," he said. "How did *you* know?"

How could I start to explain? Dad still thought the drawer was jammed. I couldn't admit I'd been out and got myself soaked to the skin.

"Just . . . guessing," I said. "Thanks, Dad."

Chapter Eight

Wow-eeeh!

I rushed back to my room, threw myself on my bed and stared at the old wooden chest. I thought of the comics inside it; they weren't a patch on this business.

I wondered where the old woman had managed to hide poor Lisa while Dad was whistling about, cheerily clearing the house. Locked in a cellar perhaps, or trussed and gagged in a cupboard? But what was the point of it all? Was Lisa some sort of hostage? More likely the horrid old woman had simply flipped her lid, and now that she'd toddled off into the old people's home, Lisa had just been forgotten!

I had to find out for certain. And that meant breaking into the house.

Chapter Nine

I waited till after tea, then said my cold felt worse and started up the stairs. Mum took my temperature and made me a hot lemon drink. She brought me a hot water bottle and tucked me up in bed.

I almost wished I could have stayed there, but after half an hour Dad had turned on the telly and Mum was doing her sewing. "Bzzz-zzzaaaa" went the sewing machine, "yaw-yaw" went the evening news. I got up and tiptoed downstairs to put on my damp anorak.

Setting off at a jog, I got to Rosewood
Gardens more quickly than I would have
liked.

The house looked gloomy and frightening; there weren't any lights on upstairs.

Round the back of the house, I pressed my face to a window trying to peer inside, but it was too dark to see. I managed to stifle a sneeze, then gave the window a tug. I didn't expect it to budge but the catch tore out of the wood. Suddenly, with a great screech, the old wooden sash shot up, leaving me plenty of room to clamber over the sill.

I was halfway through the window, one leg in, one out, when I thought I heard voices. I stopped. I leant back into the garden but then I could only hear traffic. The noises inside were different. I leant forwards into the room and . . .

Something hit me hard – thump – on the head.

My knees buckled.

Chapter Ten

I woke up flat on the floor. My hands and chin were scratched. My head was buzzing with stars and, though my ears were ringing, I heard those voices again. This time they sounded much closer – in the next room. They were laughing.

How long had I been knocked out? I peered at my watch. Ten minutes?

Feeling shaky I got to my feet, but when I turned back to the window I found it was shut. Then I clicked. The window had slammed on my head. I pushed it, heaved it and wrenched it, but the window was jammed.

Don't panic. Breathe slowly. Think fast.

There was only one other way out – through the doorway into the hall. And someone might be in the hall.

At least the door wasn't locked. Edging it open a little, I took a long careful look. A streetlamp cast a faint glow through a stained glass window above the dark front door. That was okay. That was normal. It showed me the hallway was empty.

What got me spooked was a beam of shivery, yellowish light which came from a door on my left. This door was open a crack. As I inched into the hall I took a quick look. My heart lurched.

The front room was crowded with candles, all flickering in the draught with big, fat, buttery flames that sent enormous shadows wandering over the walls. And on the mantelpiece was a giant, hollowed-out pumpkin with slits for eyes and mouth.

What was going on here?

Chapter Eleven

I still couldn't see any people, but what I could hear chilled my bones.

"We're creatures out of the past who are haunting this house for an hour . . ."

I took a step back. My mistake. My foot banged into the door-frame, triggering total chaos.

"Calm down," said the grown-up voice. "*We're* the spooks, we're doing the haunting. So let's take a look, shall we?"

The door was tugged open. She saw me straight away.

I could hardly believe it. The woman wore heavy black clothes. Her long flowing skirts brushed the floorboards with a dry, rasping noise. Her hand closed cold round my wrist.

Chapter Twelve

"Who are you?" she asked, not unkindly, though not letting go of my wrist.

"I'm P-PP P-PP Pete."

"I don't think we've met before, Pete. I take it you were invited?"

"Just looking for someone," I mumbled.

"Not Lisa?" called one of the children.

I didn't know what to say. If they had captured Lisa they'd capture me too, and then what? While I was trying to think straight, I was pulled into the room.

Inside there were two more women, also wearing black, and maybe a dozen children. But what really gave me the wobblies was the fact that the girls were dressed exactly like the girl in my photograph!

"Who asked you to come?" said the woman.

I kept my mouth shut.

"Well? We saw you out in the street in the rain."

"It's time!" shouted one of the children.

"Too soon!" said one of the women.

"We've counted a hundred and fifty."

"All right, Pete, since you're here, would you like to help find Lisa?"

I nodded, feeling even more confused. Lisa was here, but they'd lost her? The woman let go of my wrist.

"Ready, set, GO!" We were off.

The children were wailing and screeching, "Lisa, we'll catch you, we'll get you". But on the first-floor landing they fanned out in all directions, leaving me by myself. I dashed on up the stairs, all the way to the top floor.

I knew I wouldn't have long.

Chapter Thirteen

It wasn't all dark up
there. Candles
spluttered in jam jars
between the bannister
rails, making horrible
shadows that wobbled
and wandered like
ghosts.

At the top of the stairs
I faltered, facing three
closed doors. I worked
out which one I
wanted, but would it
be locked?

I gave the handle a twist. The door
was stuck, so I barged it, giving it such a
thump that it banged hard back on its
hinges. Inside was a small shabby room,
lit by a couple of candles.

The room was completely empty. I
sneezed with relief. But hang on. That's
when I heard an odd noise, a low sort of
laugh . . . or a sob. Where from? I looked
round more carefully, feeling my stomach
clench tight.

Grey marks on the faded wallpaper
showed where some pictures had hung
and where my chest must have been. But
to the left of the window I saw something
else: a low door, the entrance to a
cupboard under the eaves of the roof.

On tiptoe I moved towards it. I pressed
one ear to the wood. The blood in my
head was roaring but I heard something
shift in the cupboard. It shuffled, then it
. . . coughed.

I tugged the door open wide.

Chapter Fourteen

It was her. The girl at the window.
And now I could see for a fact
that she *was* the girl in the photo,
wearing the same old clothes.
But her face was
deathly white.

I tottered backwards.

I heard her gasp, "Who are you?"

"I found your note," I said wildly. "About being lonely and ill, and here I am. You *are* Lisa?"

She jerked her head. She looked crazy.

"We'll have to be quick though," I whispered. "They're coming. We'll fight our way out."

She opened her eyes extra wide. "You think you can spook me, don't you?"

"What, me? It's those ghosts, downstairs. I'm not one of them, I'm a friend, I . . ."

The children were closing in fast.

I tried to grab hold of her arm, but she ducked back into the cupboard. The children burst into the room, baying like wolves. They closed round me.

I lashed out with fists and feet and managed to fend them off, but as I swung round for Lisa, she opened her mouth and . . . laughed.

Only then did I understand that she was one of *them*!

Forcing my way to the landing, I practically skied down the staircase, the rest of the children behind me, screaming and calling my name. I hit the front door at full tilt and fumbled to undo the catch. A woman in black rushed towards me but I managed to push her away, then I was out of the doorway and over the garden wall.

I didn't stop till I reached home.

Mum heard me on the stairs, but I was safely in bed before her head appeared round my bedroom door.

"Just wondering," I said rather hoarsely, "if there's any chance of some Horlicks?"

She peered at me, eyebrows raised.

I got no sleep that night. I sat up and read the note over and over again, stared at the photograph and even thumbed through the book in case I could find some more clues.

I clicked out the light. Then it hit me. I'd
been lured to a haunted house by the
note and the face at the window. Those
spooks had intended to catch me. Why?
To make *me* a spook!

I sat bolt upright in bed, switched on the
light again and stared at the chest full of
comics. I wished that I'd chucked them all
out. Then I wouldn't have needed the
chest, I'd never have opened the drawer
and I'd never have heard of Lisa. But
thinking like this didn't help. I needed to
talk to someone.

If I talked to my parents they'd laugh.
Who would believe me? Only someone
who'd lived in that house. And who was
that someone? That's right. I needed to
meet the old lady.

Chapter Sixteen

I reckoned Dad
knew the address
of the old people's
home where Mrs Tatley now
lived, but what excuse could I find
for saying I wanted to go there?

I did have her book to return – the copy
of *Peter Pan*. When I showed it to Dad and
told him that I'd found it in the chest, he
said that he'd give me a lift to the old
people's home after school.

But Dad was right, as it happens.
Mrs Tatley wasn't the frightening old hag
I'd imagined. She seemed far too gentle
and friendly to keep a girl locked in a
bedroom, or to have any dealings with
spooks. Was that why she had moved
out? If so, she was taking it calmly.

49

She clapped when I showed her the book. "Amazing! That does bring back memories. How kind of you to return it." She gave me a wonderful smile. "But what's the matter with you, dear? You look as if you've seen a ghost."

"Ghost?" Before I could tell her, a nurse came in with the tea. And while Dad was munching shortbreads, Mrs Tatley flicked through the book. She soon found the photograph.

I nodded.

"It makes quite a tale. To start with, my name's Lisa. That's me in the picture, you see?"

I swallowed. My mouth felt dry, as if it was stuffed full of carpet.

That meant I'd seen her last night.
The ghost of someone still living.
A sort of back-to-front ghost?

I did my best to speak, but only came out with a croak.

"I wrote the note too," she told me.
"A very long time ago. I wonder if you can guess why?"

She had to be joking. I waited.

"When I was about your age, a year or so younger perhaps, I suffered from scarlet fever, a nasty disease in those days. I had to be kept by myself, in quarantine, so I got lonely. No telly; I had to read.

And one of my favourite books was this one." She tapped *Peter Pan*. "I read it again and again, and one night I had a strange dream.

I dreamt that Peter Pan came to my room to see me. He'd left me a message to say that he would only return if I wrote him a letter which I should put in this book and lock in my secret drawer."

She paused to sip some tea.

"I wrote to him straight away, on the back of this picture of me."

"When he didn't come back, I had the
bright idea that maybe he was shy and he
might only return if I was asleep or not
there. So I hid in the cupboard – and then
I couldn't get out. It was terribly
frightening. I screamed till I woke my
mother, who wasn't the least bit pleased,
but Peter Pan never turned up."

"But the book," I persisted. "The book with the note and the photo. You left them in the drawer?"

"I had to. I lost the key. And then I forgot all about them. The chest stayed up in that bedroom until your father took it."

"Well, well . . ." Dad took the last shortbread. "What an odd tale, Mrs Tatley. But have you thought?" His eyes glistened. "Pete here's been your Peter Pan!"

Exactly. All good wishes come true in the end.

But-but I saw your ghost last night. The ghost of you when you were young. And when I tried to help you, the other ghosts all attacked me and then you were on their side.

Dad practically spat out his shortbread. "What *are* you talking about, Pete?"

Before I could say any more, we heard a loud knock on the door.

Mrs Tatley said, "Pete, would you kindly . . . ?"

So I opened the door and got the shock of my life.

Chapter Seventeen

I groaned. I stumbled backwards. "It's *her*!" I burbled, "It's Lisa. I mean . . . the other Lisa!"

It's him, Mummy— the boy that tried to scare me.

"What is this?" I managed.

"My dear . . ." The old lady looked really pleased. "This is my great granddaughter, whose name, as you say, is my own. And doesn't she look just like I did, eighty-five years ago?"

"We met last night," said the mother, who had come in behind Lisa. She was wearing jeans and a sweater instead of her long black skirts.

I started to feel rather dizzy.

"We gave him a fright," Lisa said. "I laughed and he ran. What a baby!"

Dad clanked his cup down in his saucer.

So Lisa and her mother told Dad about
how they had seen me, early that
afternoon, out in the street, soaking wet.
And how I had gatecrashed their party.

It made me look pretty stupid.
I was shrinking inside.
Dad looked rather queasy, as if
he'd had too many shortbreads.

"Peter," he said, rather gruffly. "I don't
think I'm hearing correctly."

Top marks for logic.

59

"Yes, what was *she* doing?" said Dad.

"My fault," said Lisa's mother. "I thought it would be more spooky holding a Halloween party in Granny's empty house. We were playing hide-and-seek. And thanks to Granny's old story about getting locked in the cupboard, that's where Lisa wanted to hide."

But in those weird clothes?

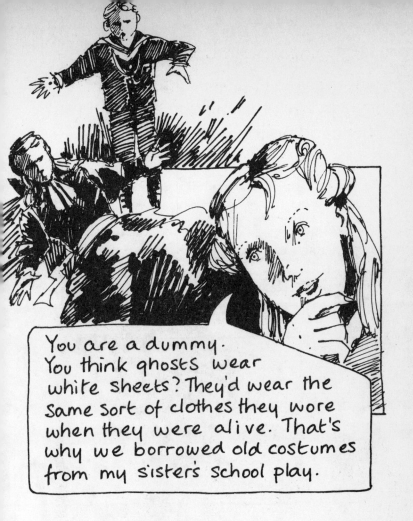

You are a dummy.
You think ghosts wear
white sheets? They'd wear the
same sort of clothes they wore
when they were alive. That's
why we borrowed old costumes
from my sister's school play.

"So that's it," said Lisa's mother. "The
mystery is solved."

"But that's not all," Mrs Tatley d_____ ___
in a cheery voice. "Oh no, you'v_____
out the best bits!

"How well things have come together!
Pete brought Lisa's party to life. He
brought back this old book which I can
now hand on to Lisa.

"And, on top of all that, I've finally met Peter Pan. He seems such a very nice chap, I do hope that we shall be friends."

"Now who's a dummy?" her mum said.

"It's . . . complicated," said Dad.

"And," said Mrs Tatley, "Pete still hasn't had any tea. I think we might ask for more biscuits. I take it you do like shortbreads?"

"Oh yes," Dad said at once. So I just nodded and grinned.